FACT:

John broadcast the first live outside event. It was a horse race called the Epsom Derby.

FACT:

John opened his own television company in a building called The Crystal Palace in London. He made televisors for people to buy and transmitted live pictures of dancers and actors for them to watch on their new machines.

FACT:

When World War II began, all British television shut down. John had to sell his company - no one wanted to buy any televisions because there were no programs to watch.

FACT:

During the war John helped develop fibre optics, radar, infrared night viewing devices and secret signaling.

FACT:

In 1936 The Crystal Palace burnt down. John lost nearly all his equipment.

This book belongs to...

_____

_____

_____

_____

Mister T.V.
An original concept by author Julie Fulton
© Julie Fulton
Illustrated by Patrick Corrigan

MAVERICK ARTS PUBLISHING LTD
Studio 11, City Business Centre, 6 Brighton Road, Horsham,
West Sussex, RH13 5BB, +44 (0)1403 256941

First Published in the UK in 2020 by
MAVERICK ARTS PUBLISHING LTD

American edition published in 2020 by Maverick Arts Publishing, distributed in the United States and
Canada by Lerner Publishing Group Inc., 241 First Avenue North, Minneapolis, MN 55401 USA

ISBN 978-1-84886-646-1

www.maverickbooks.co.uk

1856

The first practical fax machine, working on telegraph lines, was developed and put into service by the Italian priest Giovanni Caselli.

1873

Willoughby Smith, an English electrical engineer, discovers the photoconductivity of the element selenium.

1885

Paul Gottlieb Nipkow creates an image scanning device, later called 'Nipkow's disk'.

Tele-timeline!

(Inventions that Helped Make T.V. Possible)

MISTER T.V.

Written by Julie Fulton
Illustrated by Patrick Corrigan

1900

The word 'television' coined by Constantin Perskyi at the International Electricity Congress at the International World Fair.

The first demonstration of the instantaneous transmission of still images by Georges Rignoux and A. Fournier in Paris.

1909

1926

John Logie Baird demonstrates his working televisor, a mechanical television that showed live, moving images.

This is **John**.

John lived with his family in Helensburgh, Scotland in a house full of books. Sometimes John was too ill to go and play with his friends, but he wanted to talk with them.

I wonder...

"I'll **invent** something," he said and
started to collect bits and pieces.

Soon John had linked up telephones from his house to his friends' houses.

FACT:
The real telephone company found out about John's home-made telephone exchange and made him stop.

But, one night, a storm blew down one of the lines. It knocked the driver of a horse-drawn cab from his seat.

John had to find something else to do.

"It's hard to read by gaslight," said John. "We need brighter lights."
He started to collect bits and pieces.

I wonder...

Before long, he'd built a machine to make electricity for his home.

But, one night, the machine stopped working! The lights went out. John's father fell down the stairs.

That didn't work...

FACT:

John's machine was called a generator. He used all sorts of things, including jam jars, to make it.

When John was older, he had to get a job but he really wanted to keep inventing.

I wonder...

He started to collect bits and pieces.

THE DIAMOND MAKER

FACT:

One of the stories John read as a boy said you could make diamonds if you had lots of electricity. And, working in an electricity generating factory, John had loads! He decided to see if he really could make his own diamonds.

But John's experiment went wrong. All the electricity went off in Glasgow.
Machinery in factories and shipyards stopped working. Lights went out.
People bumped into each other in the dark.

He thought a lot and he tried making different things.
Some things didn't work.

Like a **glass razor** that wouldn't rust.

And shoes filled with **air** for comfort.

But some things did. John's **special socks** helped people keep their feet dry in Glasgow's wet weather. **But...**

All the hard work made John ill. His doctor sent him to the seaside to get better. John read about an inventor who tried to build machines that showed **real live pictures** to people in their homes.

I wonder...

"I could build these machines and make them work," said John.
He started to collect bits and pieces.

John tried and he tried and one day his machines were ready.
He placed a large cross in front of his special transmitting machine, then peered at the screen on his receiving machine.

"It works!" he said. "But the picture's fuzzy.
I'll make it better."

FACT:

John didn't have much money. He had to use what he could find – an old electric motor, a hat box, a biscuit tin, a bicycle lamp, batteries, a needle, string and wax.

John tried and tried again. One day, his machines got **too hot**. They exploded and burnt his hand.

After much more hard work, he placed a doll's head
under the lights and ran to the screen.

"It works! The picture's clearer. I must try with a real person!"
John raced downstairs.

He grabbed the first person he saw and sat him under the hot lights.

"Turn your head," shouted John, looking at the screen.
The man turned his head.

"Open your mouth."

"It works! I can see you moving!"

 **FACT:**

The man was called William Taynton. In 1925 he became the first ever person to be seen on television - even if it was only by John!

Scientists queued up outside John's workshop to see his machines.
"I call this my **televisor**," said John. "One day it will be as normal to have in your house as a radio is today."

FACT:

This was the first time live, moving pictures were shown in public. Today we use the word 'television'. It means 'far seeing'.

John tried and he tried and his televisor got better and better.
He sent live pictures from **London** to screens in **Glasgow** and
New York.

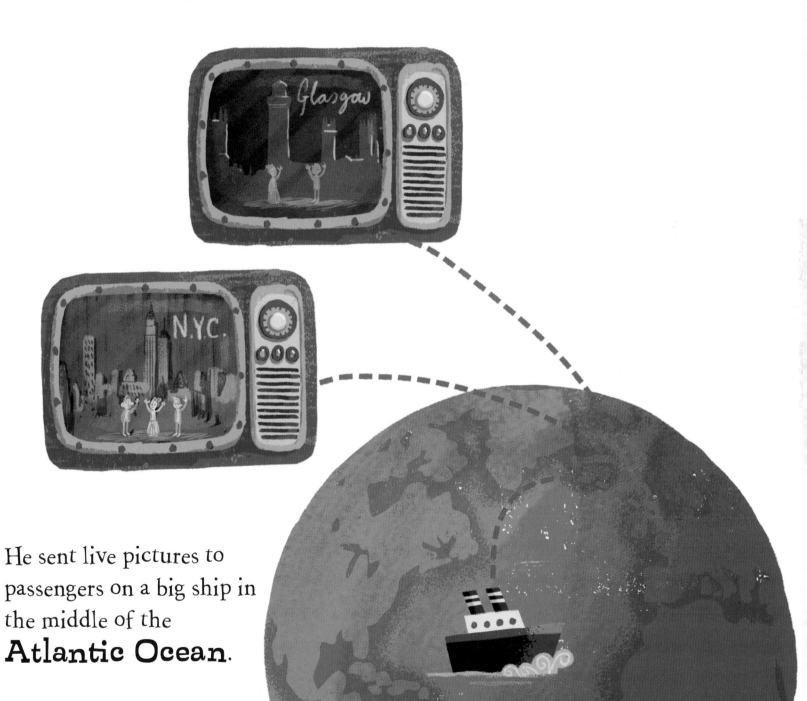

He sent live pictures to
passengers on a big ship in
the middle of the
Atlantic Ocean.

John even sent live performances to people's homes.

FACT:

When the British Broadcasting Corporation started making programs in 1929 they used John's machines.

When the Prime Minister was given a televisor, John felt very proud.

What do you mean there are only **three programs a week?**

FACT:

This was true! The BBC only broadcasted three 15 minute programs a week.

John never gave up inventing. He was always collecting bits and pieces to make his inventions better and better.

FACT:

John was the first man to transmit color pictures. He really did invent 3D T.V.

John was right about **television** too. It's such a normal part of our lives it's hard to imagine a time when it didn't exist. And, just as John would have wanted, it's getting better and better every day.

The Baird Televisor

Author's Note:

John Logie Baird was a Scottish engineer and known as one of the inventors of the mechanical television. He was never called Mister T.V. but he should have been as without him television would not be what it is today.

John wasn't the only person working hard to build a television. In the early 20th century, more than 50 inventors from around the world were trying to do the same. They included Farnsworth and Jenkins in America; Zworykin and Theremin in Russia; Takayanagi in Japan; Rignoux and Fournier in France. But John built the very first working mechanical T.V. and was the first person to transmit live, moving pictures.

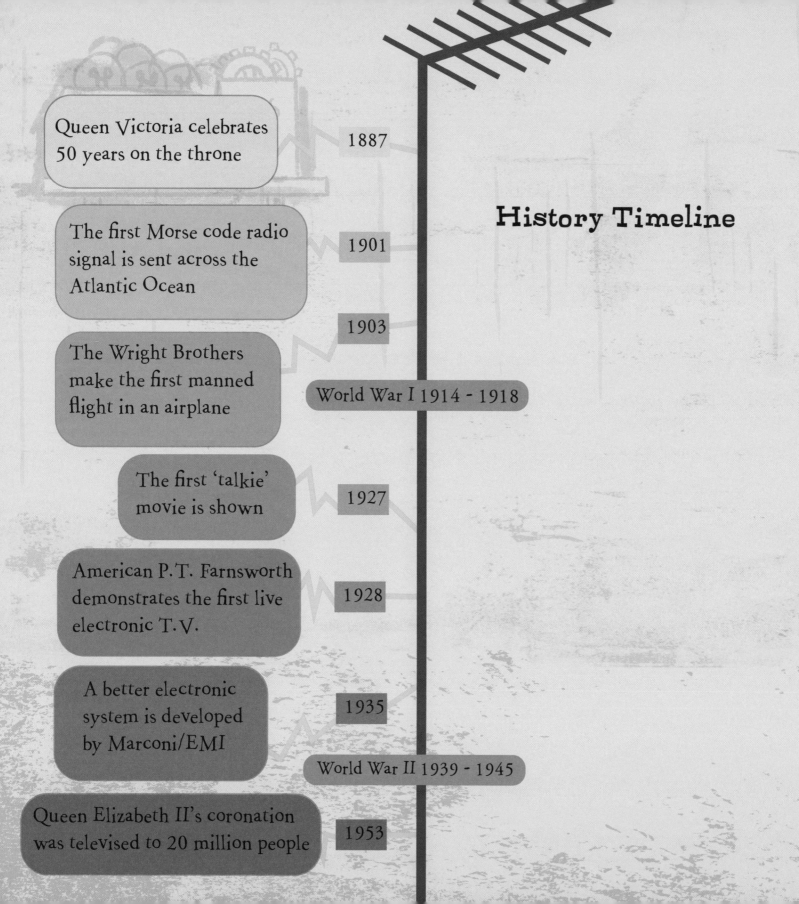

History Timeline

Queen Victoria celebrates 50 years on the throne — **1887**

The first Morse code radio signal is sent across the Atlantic Ocean — **1901**

1903

The Wright Brothers make the first manned flight in an airplane

World War I 1914 - 1918

'The first 'talkie' movie is shown — **1927**

American P.T. Farnsworth demonstrates the first live electronic T.V. — **1928**

A better electronic system is developed by Marconi/EMI — **1935**

World War II 1939 - 1945

Queen Elizabeth II's coronation was televised to 20 million people — **1953**